Published in the UK in 2025 by Post Wave Children's Books,
an imprint of Post Wave Publishing UK Ltd,
Runway East, 24-28 Bloomsbury Way, London, WC1A 2SN
www.postwavepublishing.com

First edition 1997
Published with permission of Gallimard Jeunesse
Original title: *La Nature Au Fil Des Mois*
Written and illustrated by René Mettler
Consulted by Camilla de la Bedoyere
Copyright @ Gallimard Jeunesse, France, 1997
www.gallimard-jeunesse.fr

A catalogue record of this book is available from the British Library.

10 9 8 7 6 5 4 3 2 1

ISBN 978-1-83627-009-6

Printed in China

MIX
Paper | Supporting
responsible forestry
FSC
www.fsc.org
FSC® C020056

A
Year
in
Nature

René Mettler

A Year in Nature

Explore the countryside,
month by month

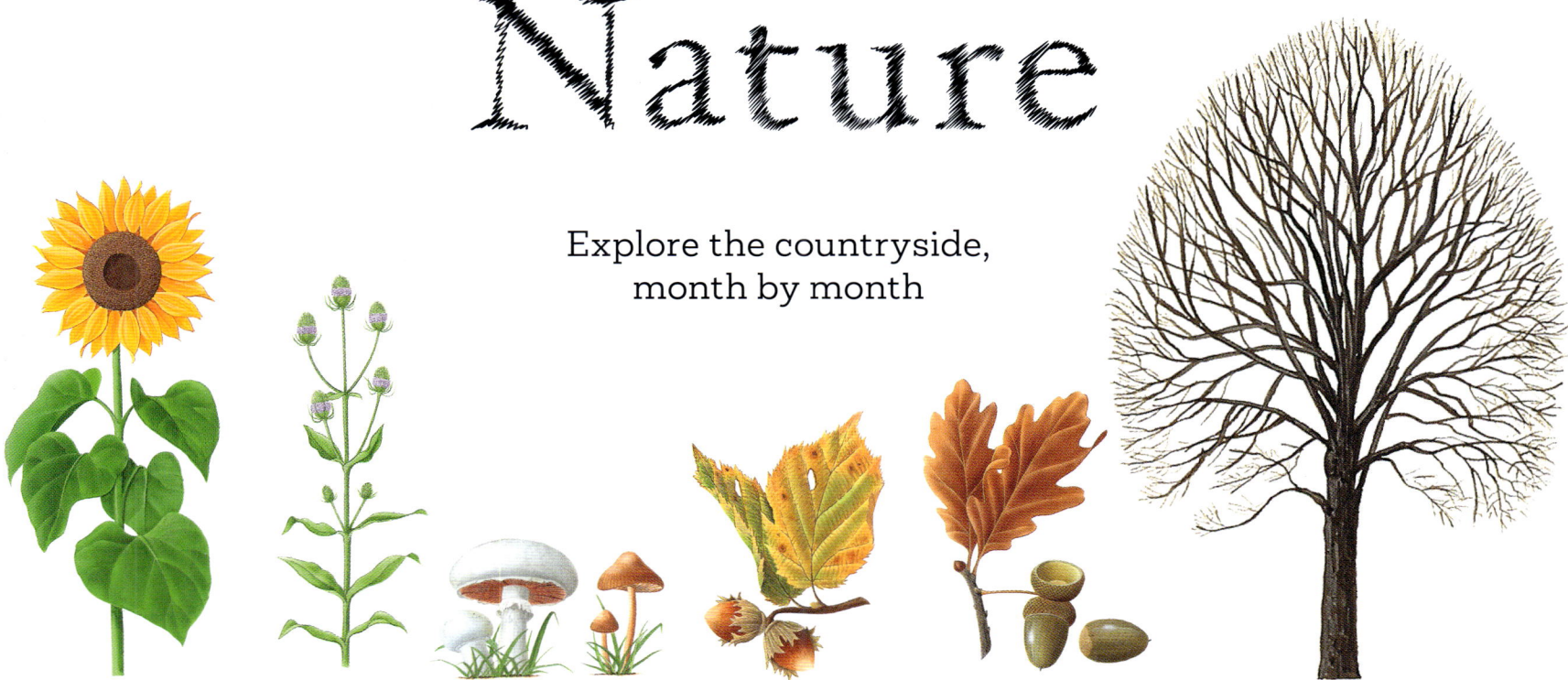

post wave

THE SEASONS

Seasons are like Earth's natural clock, telling us what time of year it is. Understanding the seasons helps us to plan activities, slow down and appreciate what is happening all around us in nature. In Europe and many other regions, the seasons alternate from hot to cold, changing gradually throughout the year. Nature adapts to this cycle.

The Earth rotates around an axis inclined at around 23.5 degrees.

In spring when the weather gets warmer, plants wake up from their sleep and start growing. Plants need solar energy from the sun to survive, and when the first fine days of spring arrive, they start to grow quickly. Animals start to have babies, who grow bigger and stronger over the course of the year, before the harsh winter sets in.

In the summer, when the weather really heats up, plants begin to produce fruits and seeds. Farmers work hard to grow crops like corn and tomatoes, ready to be picked at the end of the season. When autumn comes around, the temperature cools and the leaves on the trees change colour. Plants begin to slow down their activity, while farmers harvest their crops. Some animals enter hibernation, sleeping for most of the season. Winter is when nature takes a rest.

From plants to animals, every part of nature evolves with the seasons, and we can see this in the landscape before us.

JANUARY 14th

The year usually starts when it is cold, quite often when temperatures are below freezing. Lakes and other water bodies turn to ice, except for streams and rivers, where the constant flow of water prevents ice from forming.

Snow falls and settles on the cold ground. First, it dusts the open fields, then it turns everything white. Animals need maximum energy to stay warm during this time and the hard frost makes it difficult to collect food, which is already in short supply.

The Gardener's Basket

We harvest: Brussels sprouts; winter cabbage; lamb's lettuce; winter leeks; black salsify.

January 14th
3pm

Winter is a very difficult time for birds. When food is scarce, the berries left on the shrubs, as well as a few flower seeds, are a welcome treat.

Great tit

Robin

2 Snowflakes are tiny ice crystals that form when water vapour freezes into ice around specks of dust or pollen floating in the air.

1 To combat the cold, birds puff up their feathers, trapping a layer of air that insulates their bodies.

4 The brimstone butterfly spends winter in a state of lethargy, often hiding in tree holes, nestled in the cavity of a rock or simply sheltered by a dead leaf.

3 Thrushes belong to the same family as blackbirds – the Turdidae family. They are a common sight in winter. Assembled in troops, they often feed on berries. Mistle thrushes are particularly fond of mistletoe, helping it to be dispersed over the countryside.

Mistle thrush

Fieldfare

5 The daisy is a very common little plant. It blooms all year round.

6 The fox, like many mammals, grows a much thicker coat as winter approaches to help combat the cold.

Spring runs from around March 19th to June 21st. During spring, the days are longer than the nights and the sun climbs higher and higher in the sky. Temperatures become milder.

Winter runs from around December 21st to March 20th. The sun is at its lowest point in the sky, and temperatures are low.

March 19 or 21
Known as the spring equinox, on this day daylight and night-time hours are almost equal.

June 20 or 21
This is when the longest day occurs.

December 21 or 22
This is when the longest night occurs.

September 22 or 23
Known as the autumn equinox, daylight and night-time hours are almost equal.

Summer runs from around June 21st to September 22nd. At the peak of summer, the sun reaches the highest point in the sky. The days are long and hot.

Autumn runs from around September 22nd to December 21st. The sun's position is lower in the sky. The days become shorter, and the weather becomes cooler.

The position of the Earth as it orbits around the sun, and the intensity and duration of the sunlight, causes the seasons.

In summer, the sun is high in the sky. Because Earth is leaning towards the sun, its rays are short and more intense, retaining their heat.

In winter, the sun is low in the sky. Because Earth is tilted farther away, its rays are longer, reducing their strength.

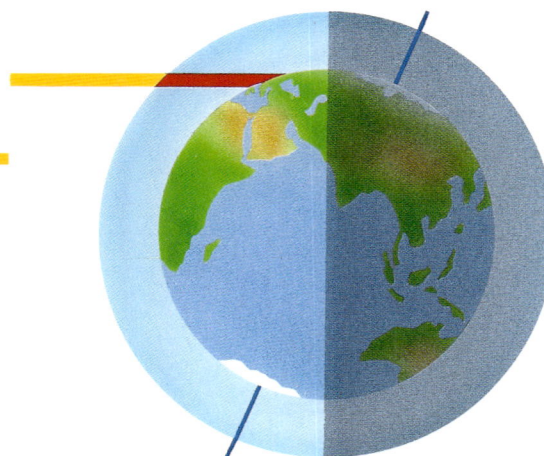

FEBRUARY 17th

Time: 12pm

Temperature: -8°C

Day/Night

The snow totally transforms the look of the countryside, blanketing the landscape and giving the trees and hillside gentle, soft lines. Anything that has not been covered stands out against the white background, creating strong contrasts.

The snow doesn't freeze the ground, as you might expect. It actually insulates the earth against very cold weather by keeping heat in and preventing water from evaporating. This helps to maintain a ground temperature just below zero.

The snow does however create an additional obstacle for animals who feed on the ground. Some will be too weak to survive the harshness of winter.

The Gardener's Basket

We continue to harvest: Brussels sprouts;
winter cabbage; lamb's lettuce; winter leeks; black salsify.
To combat the shortage of vegetables, we can rely
on preserves made in times of plenty.

Rabbit   Fox   Stoat

④ ⑤ ② ③ ①

We can help birds get through the winter by filling bird feeders with plain, unsalted peanuts.

① Snow cover provides an excellent opportunity to observe animal tracks. A rabbit's tracks are easy to identify because its hind paws create longer footprints than its front paws.

② The chattering magpie, with its beautiful black-and-white plumage and shimmering metallic greens and blues, stands out against the snow. In winter, it likes to travel in small flocks.

Stoat

Weasel

③ The stoat, and its cousin the weasel, are two of the smallest carnivores of the countryside. Apart from their size, the black tip of the stoat's tail differentiates it from the weasel, especially in winter, when both sport white coats.

④ Finches belong to the Fringillidae family, and are mostly granivores (seed-eaters). This helps them survive in the winter because they can still find food, even when it's cold and snowy.

⑤ *Yellow bunting*

Despite the blanket of snow covering the earth, the field vole is able to search for food by burrowing underground. It does not hibernate.

Greenfinch   Brambling   Bullfinch

MARCH 16th

Time: 10am

Temperature: 5°C

Day/Night

The spring equinox marks the first day of spring. On this date, day and night have the same duration. After a long winter's sleep, nature is beginning to wake up. Sap starts to rise in trees and shrubs, bringing water and sugar to flower and leaf buds, which swell and open.

The first flowers appear on hedgerows and across meadows. Farmers' fields turn green, signalling that crops such as wheat and rapeseed have resumed growing. The weather becomes warm and pleasant.

Despite the sunshine, there is often more rainfall in spring. Sudden heavy showers, combined with the melting snow, can often cause streams and rivers to burst their banks, and fields to flood.

The Gardener's Basket

We harvest: broccoli, spinach.
We continue to harvest: Brussels sprouts; winter cabbage;
lamb's lettuce; winter leeks; black salsify.

1 The blackthorn is one of the first shrubs to bloom, even before its leaves have fully developed.

2 The hedgehog is a hibernating mammal. When it wakes up in spring, it goes in search of a partner. After around 40 days, females give birth to four or five babies, called hoglets. When they are born, their spiky quills are covered with a thin layer of skin, and the quills start to appear a few hours later.

Oak   Ash   Walnut   Lime   Poplar

The position of buds on twigs, their colour, shape and number, can all be used to identify a species of tree or shrub.

3 The pussy willow is known for its soft, fluffy flower buds, or catkins, which look like a cat's paws. The catkins provide pollen for bees and other insects at a time when there are few other flowers for them to visit.

4 Cowslip is one of the first flowers of the year. Its scientific name is *Primula veris*, from the Latin '*primulus*' meaning 'the very first', and '*veris*' meaning 'spring'.

5 The brimstone butterfly, which has spent the winter resting under a leaf, spreads its wings and flies off as soon as the weather warms up.

6 The blackbird is one of the first birds to nest and lay eggs. The male is easily recognised by its black plumage and bright yellow beak. Females are a similar shape and size, but have brown, speckled plumage.

Flowers of the Month

Dandelion   Speedwell   Lesser celandine   Pansy   Violet

7 The lapwing can be found in damp meadows and floodplains, where it builds its nest on the ground. During courtship, it puts on an acrobatic display in flight, flashing its black and white wings.

APRIL 15th

Nature is stirring to life once more. Spring brings luscious greenery with newly unfurled leaves revealing their fresh, vibrant colours of yellow, green, red and rich brown, depending on the species. Fruit trees are laden with clouds of spectacular white or pink blossom. Yellow rapeseed flowers begin to bloom and wheat turns a darker green.

Migratory birds are starting to return. Among them are swallows who have travelled from as far away as Africa. Although the weather is milder, there is still a chance of sub-zero temperatures, which can freeze the flowers of fruit trees and compromise the future harvest.

The Gardener's Basket

We harvest: lettuce; white onions; radish.
We continue to harvest: broccoli; Brussels sprouts; cabbages; spinach.

1 *Apple blossom*

Each species of bird has its own technique for nest-building. There is therefore a huge variety of shapes and materials used. Factors such as the environment and behaviours of potential predators determine where the nest will be built.

2 The whinchat builds its nest on the ground, hidden under a bush or a large tuft of grass.

3 The blackcap builds cup-shaped nests in shrubs and hedges.

4 Female chaffinches build their nests wedged in the fork of a tree, at a height of 3 to 8 metres. Males choose the nesting site.

5 All swallows are migratory birds. Many species leave Europe in the autumn to spend the winter in Africa and return in the spring. Others travel from North America to Central and South America.

Male

Female

The tree buds gradually open and spread. New leaves of all shapes and sizes unfurl. They are very different from one tree to another.

Barn swallow

House martin

Swift

The swift, which looks like a large swallow, is in fact not a member of the same family.

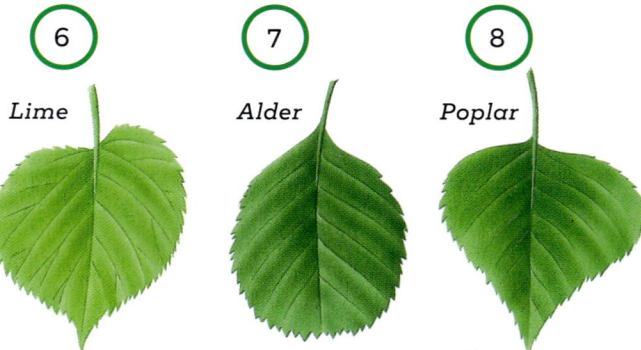

6 *Lime*

7 *Alder*

8 *Poplar*

Flowers of the Month

Forget-me-not

Herb Robert

Rabelera

9 *Oak*

11 *Field maple*

12 Cuckoo flower

13 Red deadnettle

10 *White willow*

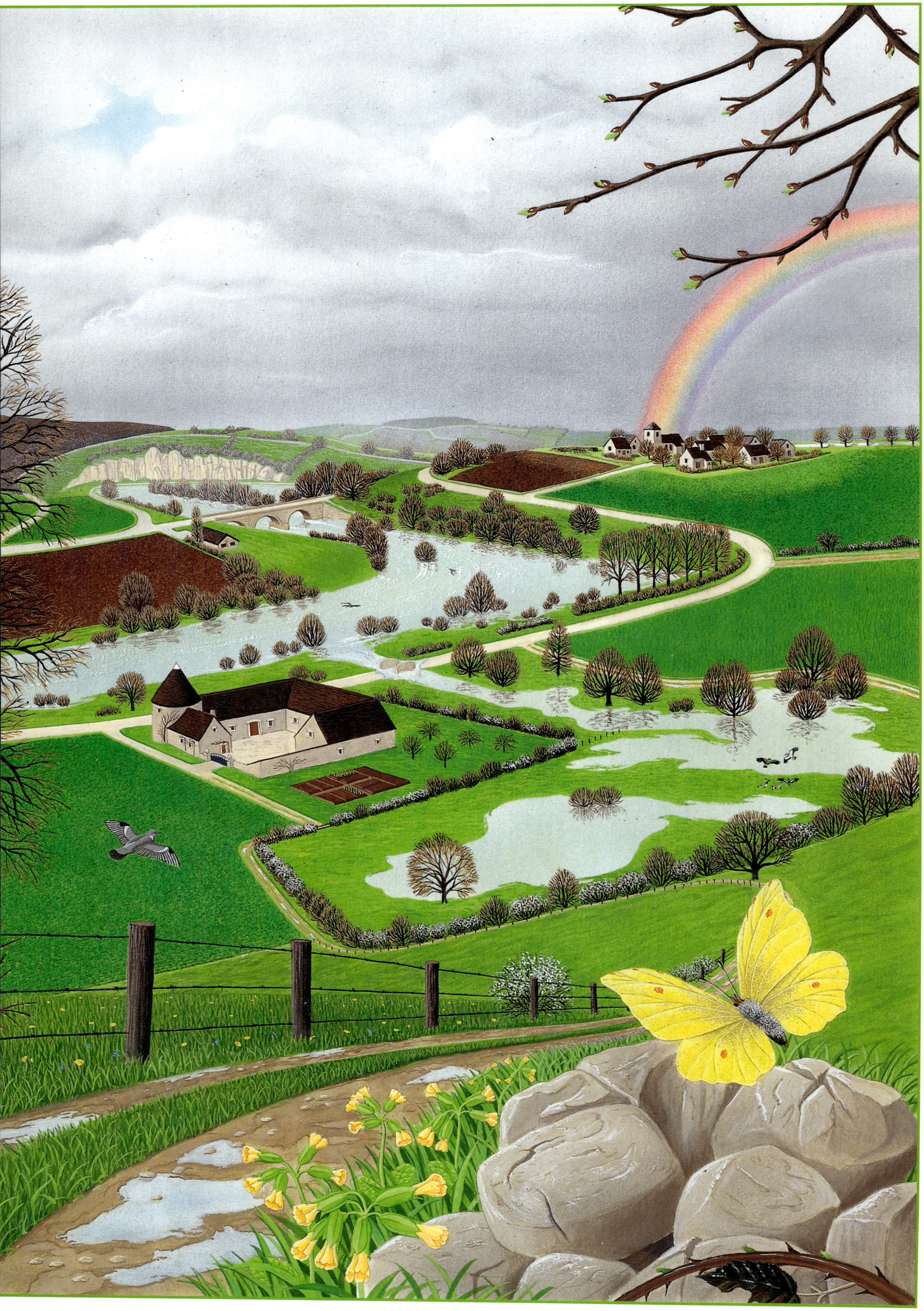

MAY 17th

Time: 9am

Temperature: 14°C

Day/Night

In just a few weeks, the trees have regrown their leaves. In meadows and along country paths, flowers attract honeybees and bumblebees. Pretty hawthorn blossom decorates hedges in delicate pinks and whites, and the flowers of rapeseed paint the fields in a brilliant yellow as they bloom in their thousands. Chicks chirp in nests, while their parents fly back and forth, bringing them insects to feast on.

The days are considerably longer, and the temperature is rising. Once again, it feels good to be outside.

The Gardener's Basket

We harvest: asparagus; strawberries; peas.
We continue to harvest: broccoli; spinach;
lettuce; white onions, radish.

May 17th
9am

1 Rapeseed, whose bright yellow flowers give the fields their colour, is widely cultivated for cooking oil, which is made by compressing the seeds.

Honeybee

3 Honeybees are key pollinators. When a honeybee enters a flower to collect nectar, a little bit of pollen is deposited onto its body. As it moves between flowers, it transfers pollen to the stigma, enabling fertilisation.

Bumblebee

Wasp

Hornet

4 Many insects, including bees, wasps and flies, pollinate flowers. They are attracted to a flower's scent and its bright colours.

7 The hoopoe is only found in Europe from April to September. Its trademark call is a deep 'hou-pou' sound, which inspired its Latin name '*Upupa*'. Its striped plumage, crest of feathers and long, curved beak make it look like an exotic bird.

2 Stalks of wheat multiply from the first shoot. A single seed will yield several ears of corn.

5 Hawthorne, also known as whitethorn, can form barriers impassable to livestock. It grows very dense, and, like blackthorn, its branches have sharp thorns.

6 Chafer beetles usually feed on leaves. Their grubs, or larvae, often live underground or in compost heaps, where they feast on dung or rotting plants. Some types of chafer beetle eat roots, damaging the plants.

9 The goldfinch deserves the term 'elegant'. It is one of the most colourful birds of the countryside.

8 Like the hoopoe, the oriole is a migratory bird. It leaves central and southern Africa to come and spend the summer in Europe.

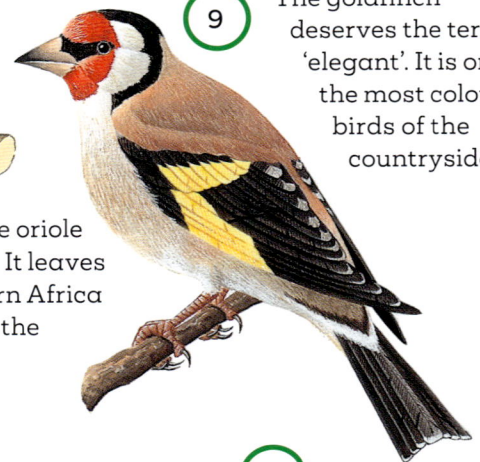

Flowers of the Month

12 Chicks beg for food by chirping with open beaks when parents approach the nest. Their colourful throats signal for food and help guide it into their mouths. Bright markings differ from one species to another.

10 Buttercup

Bladder campion

Bird's-foot trefoil

Viper's bugloss

11 Dove's foot cranesbill

JUNE 16th

This month sees the longest day of the year, marking the start of summer. Fine weather is often the order of the day and temperatures are starting to feel summery. Once the flowers have bloomed, the rapeseed fields turn pale, and look similar to ripening wheat. The landscape is dominated by green hues against which the yellow straw of the barley fields stands out – this cereal crop ripens first.

A multitude of colourful butterflies and other insects mingle with the flowers scattered in the tall grass.

The Gardener's Basket

We harvest: garlic; beetroot; carrots; cherries; cauliflower; raspberries; turnips; leeks; new potatoes; romaine lettuce; endives.
We continue to harvest: asparagus; spinach; strawberries; lettuce; white onions; peas; radishes.

June 16th
7pm

1 Dog roses are the most vigorous – and the most widespread – of wild roses. These plants often adorn the edges of paths with large pink flowers.

2 Lime blossom flowers, picked when they are in full bloom, can be dried to make herbal tea infusions.

3 The skylark is known for its distinctive behaviour. While singing, the males rise into the air, remaining almost motionless while high in the sky, before diving to the ground where they resume flight, still singing.

4 What we commonly call 'grass', is actually made up of a wide variety of herbaceous plants. Some are considered weeds, while others are cultivated to make hay.

Couch grass   Brome   Cat grass   Kentucky blue grass   Timothy grass

5 There are many ladybird species. The seven-spot is the best-known, and most common species. The two-spot species is a little smaller and can come in a wide variety of designs. Despite their name, the two-spot ladybird can have more than two spots, or none, and may be red or black.

Swallowtail   *Red admiral*

Comma   *Clouded yellow*   *Small tortoiseshell*

6 *Grass snake*   *Adder*

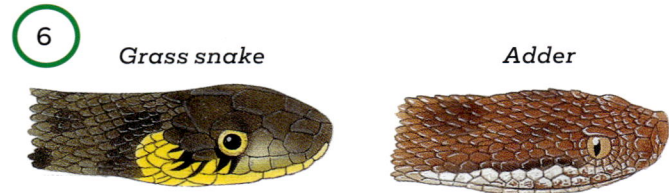

Mainly found on the banks of ponds and streams, the harmless grass snake can also be found in fields. It can easily be distinguished from the venomous adder by its rounded snout, more tapered tail and its pupil, which is round rather than slit.

Flowers of the Month

7 *Bindweed*   *Scabiosa*   *Common centaury*   *Spear thistle*   *Bellflower*

8 The peacock caterpillar feeds mainly on nettle leaves. When it has finished growing, it hangs upside-down from the plant, then splits its skin open to reveal a chrysalis. Inside, the butterfly grows. Once metamorphosis is complete, the newly formed butterfly frees itself of the chrysalis and flies away.

JULY 14th

Time: 5pm

Temperature: 25°C

Day/Night

We are now in the heart of summer. Yellow colours dominate the landscape: the rapeseed is being harvested, the wheat has ripened and thousands of sunflowers are in full bloom. The shrill chirping of grasshoppers and crickets fills the air and creates background noise in the heat.

The weather can turn stifling as the sky is quickly overtaken by large, menacing clouds. The wind intensifies. Lightning flashes, thunder roars and torrential rains or even hail follow – it's a summer storm. This dramatic display of nature's power can be dangerous. Entire harvests may be wiped out, and flash floods can cause devastating damage.

The Gardener's Basket

We harvest: apricots; chard; cabbages; apples; kohlrabi; cucmbers; courgettes; currants; green beans; melons; onions; peaches; tomatoes.
We continue to harvest: beetroot; carrots; cauliflower; spinach; lettuce; turnips; potatoes; radishes; endives.

1 Rapeseed seedpods, harvested in July, contain small seeds from which an edible oil is extracted: rapeseed oil. The residues can be made into oilcake, a protein-rich animal feed given to cattle.

2 Young sunflowers track the sun's movement across the sky, while mature sunflowers typically remain fixed facing east. Crops are harvested in September, when the flowers have set seed.

3 Soft wheat, once ground, provides flour for bread.

Rye can be used to make bread flour, as animal feed or as a source of bio-energy. Its straw was once used to cover roofs (known as thatched roofs).

Barley is referred to as malt once its grain has been soaked, allowed to sprout and then dried. Malt is one of the key ingredients in the manufacture of whisky and certain beers.

Oats are traditionally used as horse feed. Humans eat oats in the form of cereal or porridge.

Durum wheat is used to make semolina and pasta.

The sand lizard and the common wall lizard love to bask in the sun. The slow worm is not a snake, but a lizard without legs.

4

Slow worm

Common wall lizard

Umbellifers

5 Grasshoppers and locusts produce their songs by scraping spines on their legs against their wings. Crickets and katydids, such as the southern wartbiter, sing by rubbing their wings together.

Great green bush-cricket

Southern wartbiter

Brown locust

Common green grasshopper

House cricket

6 An umbellifer is a type of plant that has its flowers arranged like the ribs of an umbrella. Caution! Hemlocks are extremely toxic, and hogweed can cause allergic reactions.

Hogweed   *Hemlock*   *Fool's parsley*   *Burnet saxifrage*   *Wild carrot*

AUGUST 15th

Time: 8pm

Temperature: 28°C

Day/Night

The last of the wheat is harvested and the straw bales are brought in. The sunflower fields that were once bright are now starting to fade. The flowers droop and their yellow petals fall, turning the plants a dull shade as summer ends. The dry soil reflects the great heat of summer. The flowers at the edge of the paths are starting to become rarer. But wildflowers, mixed with herbs and umbellifers, make pretty bouquets.

Drought often lowers the water level in rivers and ponds, but, to the delight of swimmers, it remains at a pleasant temperature. For many, August is the month of vacation.

The Gardener's Basket

We harvest: aubergines; celery; cucumbers; haricot beans; plums; pears. We continue to harvest: apricots; chard; beetroot; carrots; cabbage; kohlrabi; cucumbers; courgettes; spinach; green beans; lettuce; melons; turnips; onions; peaches; leeks; potatoes; radishes; romaine lettuce; endives; tomatoes.

1 Pom-poms called bedeguar galls can be seen on rose bushes in the wild. These shaggy balls are actually scabs caused by the larvae of rose wasps.

August 15th
5pm

2 The common frog can be seen in fields and meadows, moving in small hops. It prefers to be in more humid or damp areas.

European edible dormouse

4 The barn swallow is very agile and flies at high speed, changing direction quickly to snatch small insects from the air.

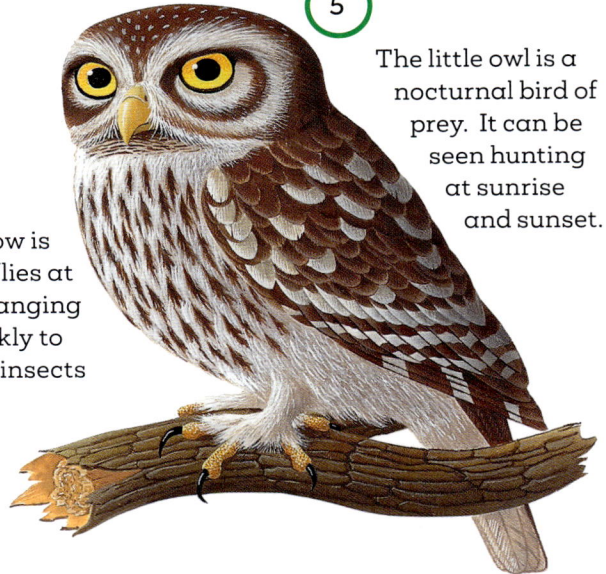

5 The little owl is a nocturnal bird of prey. It can be seen hunting at sunrise and sunset.

3 Dormice, like rats, mice and voles, are rodents. Dormice are mainly nocturnal animals, active from dusk, returning to their roosts at dawn.

Owls eat their prey whole, without chewing. Later, they cough up a pellet that contains feathers, fur and bones they couldn't digest. These pellets reveal what the owl ate and can even help to identify the species of owl.

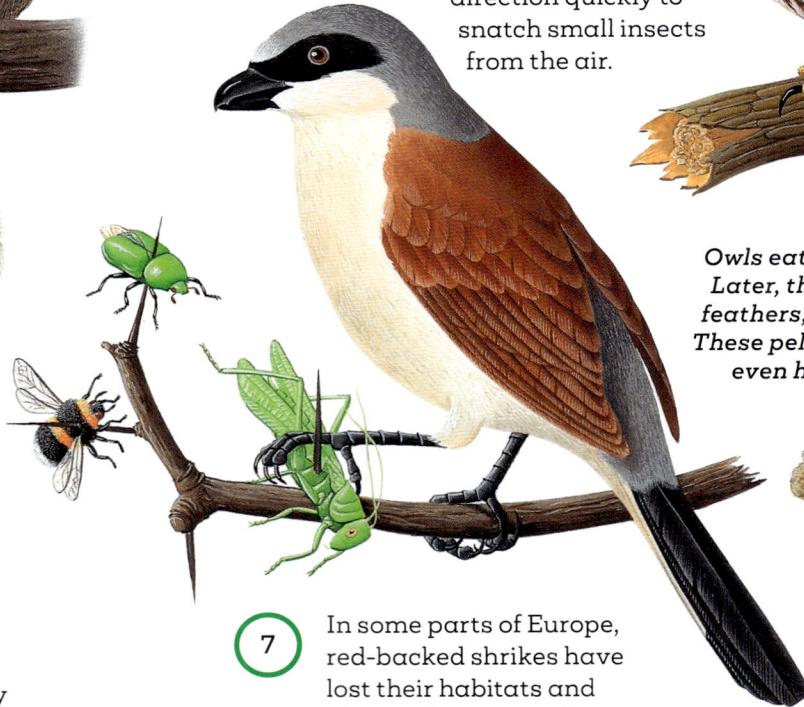

Tawny owl

Barn owl

Little owl

6 Snails dislike hot, dry weather, so they are most active on rainy days or overnight when the air is cooler.

7 In some parts of Europe, red-backed shrikes have lost their habitats and almost disappeared. Shrikes impale their prey on thorns or barbed wire.

Flowers of the Month

Grove snail

Grove snail (yellow variety)

Garden snail

Burgundy snail

Caraway

Chicory

Teasel

SEPTEMBER 14th

Time: 8am

Temperature: 11°C

Day/Night

Summer is drawing to a close. A few yellow leaves here and there herald the approach of autumn, which begins on the equinox. For the second time this year, day and night are of equal length. Nights and early mornings can be very cool with occasional fog, but the days are often still quite summery and warm.

As the sunflower harvest comes to an end, we begin to prepare the fields for future sowing. The bare earth and tired vegetation give the landscape more muted hues, but the berries that have appeared in the hedgerows add a splash of bright colour.

The Gardener's Basket

We harvest: fennel; leeks; apples; plums; grapes.
We continue to harvest: aubergines; chard; beetroots; carrots; celery; cabbage; berries; cucumbers; courgettes; spinach; haricot beans; green beans; lettuce; melons; turnips; onions; pears; potatoes; radishes; romaine lettuce; endives; tomatoes.

1

The autumn crocus is a frail and delicate flower, yet it contains a highly dangerous toxin.

2

Sunflowers are harvested once they have fully matured and all the florets on the disk have turned into seeds. These seeds are then processed to extract high-quality edible oil.

3

Spider webs are especially visible in the morning when the dew transforms their threads into strands of glistening pearls.

The European garden spider makes a beautiful, neat web. First, the female builds the outer frame and the spokes, then she finishes by spinning a perfect spiral in the middle.

4

The kestrel is a bird of prey and part of the raptor family. With sharp claws and a strong beak, it is perfectly suited for catching its prey. When hunting, the kestrel hovers in the air, carefully watching for animals on the ground. Like all raptors, kestrels can glide gracefully through the air, and the species can be identified by their unique shape when they fly.

5

The hazel dormouse is a small rodent with golden fur. Like many of its cousins, it is mainly active at night and goes back to sleep when day breaks. Its diet is almost exclusively plant-based, though it occasionally eats insects.

Common buzzard

Eurasian goshawk

Black kite

Eurasian sparrowhawk

Falcon

6

7

The blackberry is the fruit of the bramble – a shrub with long, thorny branches.

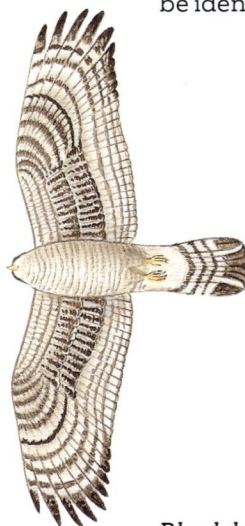

Grey partridge

Red-legged partridge

9

Agaricus campestris is a common wild mushroom.

10

Fairy ring mushrooms often grow in rows or form distinctive circles known as 'fairy rings'.

8

The grey partridge enjoys foraging for food in the hedgerows, while the red-legged partridge, found further south, prefers arid land.

OCTOBER 17th

Time: 2pm

Temperature: 13°C

Day/Night

Once again, the landscape is completely transformed. The leaves on the trees and shrubs have changed colour, with the dull greens of late summer giving way to luminous yellows, reds and oranges. These warm hues are complemented by the browns of the bare earth.

While some days remain mild, the thermometer clearly shows a drop in temperature. The first migratory birds arrive from more northerly places to spend the winter. Others leave, migrating further south in search of warmer, sunnier days.

The Gardener's Basket

We harvest: artichoke; celeriac; Brussel sprouts; cauliflowers; lamb's lettuce; walnuts; black salsify
We continue to harvest: chard; beetroots; carrots; celery; cauliflower; kohlrabi; cucumbers; courgettes; spinach; fennel; haricot beans; green beans; lettuce; pears; winter leeks; apples; radishes; grapes; tomatoes.

Walnut

11 3 4 9 2 1 8 6 5 7 10

2 *Hazelnut*

1 As winter approaches, animals gorge themselves on the season's plentiful fruits, berries and nuts. This helps them prepare for the upcoming months when food will be scarce.

3 *Hawthorne*

5 *Sloe berries*

7 The pine marten is often found in woodlands, groves and rocky terrain. This predator hunts small mammals and birds, but it is nocturnal and rarely seen.

6 *Field maple*

4 *Rosehips*

Leaves are green because of a pigment called chlorophyll. In autumn, the chlorophyll breaks down, and other pigments start to appear. These pigments range from yellow and orange to red or purple, making the leaves look vibrant and colourful.

8 A murmuration of starlings is when hundreds, or even thousands, of these birds gather together in the sky. They swirl and twist, changing direction all at once before landing in the fields.

9 Red squirrels are fond of hazelnuts. To prepare for winter, they gather large quantities and store them in various hiding spots to ensure they have enough food during the colder months.

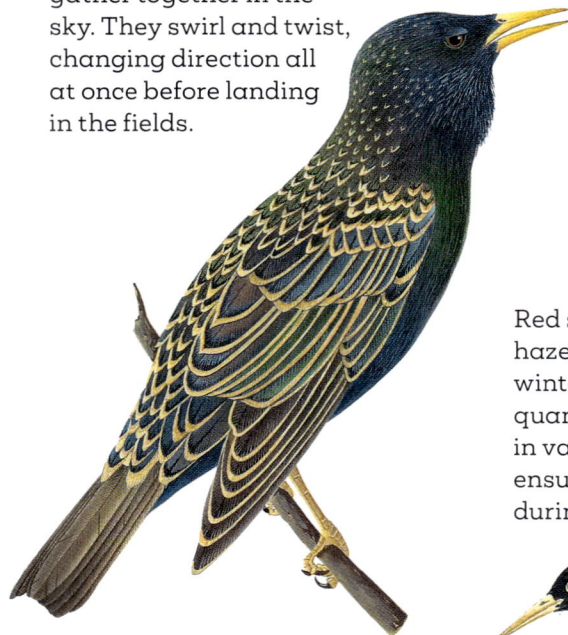

10 The mole is responsible for the mounds of earth often seen dotted around the countryside. These mounds are created from the soil that the mole digs out while making tunnels. Living entirely underground in total darkness and rarely coming to the surface, the mole has highly developed senses of smell and touch. These enhanced senses help it locate its food – insect larvae and earthworms.

11 The common crane migrates from north to south at the beginning of autumn. The flock flies in a 'V' shape, taking turns leading the pack so that the work is shared equally and no one bird becomes too tired.

NOVEMBER 16th

Time: 11am

Temperature: 6°C

Day/Night

Rain, fog and strong winds are everywhere this month. It's getting colder, and the last leaves have been plucked from the trees.

On the ground, these leaves break down thanks to tiny bacteria and other microorganisms living in the soil. The nutrients from the fallen leaves are used by plants to grow. Seeds that are spread by the wind or animals will stay in the soil until next spring, when they will begin to grow into new plants.

The Gardener's Basket

We harvest: cabbages. We continue to harvest: beetroot; artichoke thistles; carrots; celery; berries; Brussels sprouts; cauliflower; spinach; lettuce; lamb's lettuce; turnips; pears; leeks; apples; radishes; black salsify.

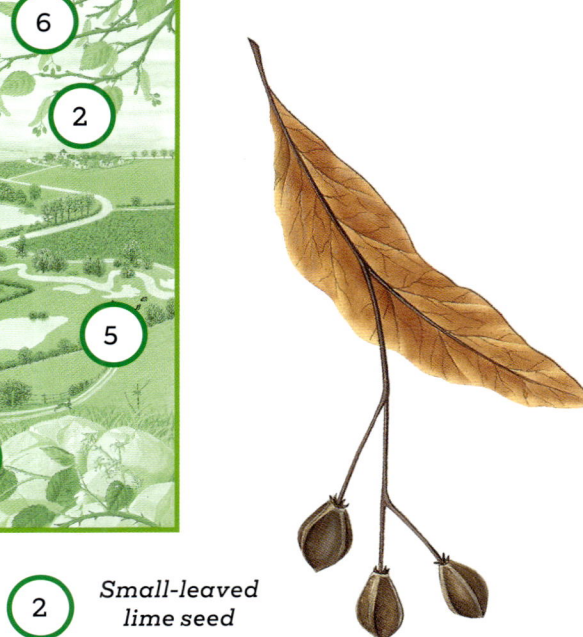

1 *Pedunculate oak acorn*

2 *Small-leaved lime seed*

Some trees use the wind to spread their seeds. These seeds often have 'wings' or other structures that help them catch the wind, allowing them to travel far from the tree where they grew.

3 The Eurasian jay spreads oak trees by gathering acorns in its beak, flying off to bury them in many places and creating a pantry for the winter. However, it doesn't always remember all of its hiding spots. The forgotten acorns therefore start to grow into new trees.

Carrion crow

4 Rooks gather in colonies, filling the tops of large trees and noisily calling to one another. They also work together in groups to search for earthworms in freshly ploughed fields. The carrion crow is often seen with rooks, which can be distinguished by their whitish beaks and the looser feathers at the base of their legs.

5 *Field maple seed pod*

Rook

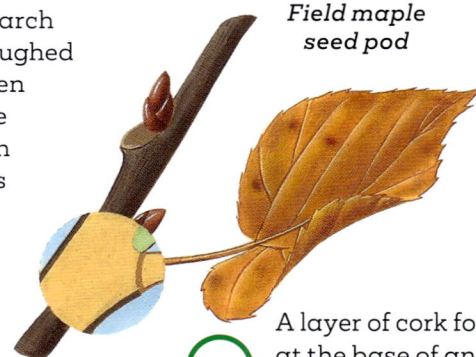

6 A layer of cork forms at the base of an aging leaf. This cork layer cuts off the supply of water and nutrients to the leaf, causing it to die and fall off. Once the leaf falls, it leaves space for a bud that will grow into a new leaf next spring.

7 The pheasant was introduced to parts of Europe by the Romans, and it is a very popular game bird. The pheasants that we encounter in the countryside are not always wild. A large number are bred on farms and are released for hunting.

With the first hint of cold weather, the hazel dormouse, European dormouse and garden dormouse will retreat to their burrows – either in a tree hole or rocky cavity – to spend the winter months there, plunged into a deep sleep known as hibernation. They spent the autumn gorging on food in order to build up fat reserves to survive without food.

DECEMBER 15th

Time: 1pm

Temperature: 5°C

Day/Night

As the days shorten, culminating on the solstice, winter officially begins with the shortest day of the year. Nature enters a state of rest. Trees and shrubs have shed their leaves, and their sap flow nearly halts, allowing them to withstand the frost without harm. Despite the harsh weather, a few resilient flowers continue to bloom here and there.

Food for animals becomes scarcer, except on sunny days when the sun melts any frost, making it easier to forage. However, as long as the ground remains free from snow, they will always manage to find something to eat.

The Gardener's Basket

We continue to harvest: carrots; celery; celeriac; Brussels sprouts; cabbage; spinach; lamb's lettuce; leeks; black salsify.

1

Winter rapeseed seeds, sown in late August to early September, will endure the winter and resume growth in the spring.

2

Small winter wheat plants blanket the fields, creating the appearance of vast green lawns stretching across the landscape. They will stay this size during the cold season, resuming their growth in the spring.

3

Mistletoe becomes visible when the leaves on the trees have fallen. This parasitic shrub stays green all year round and grows on the branches of certain soft-wooded trees, such as poplars. Being parasitic means it takes nutrients from the tree's sap to survive.

4

The male flowers of the hazel (known as catkins) begin to develop in summer and stay on the tree all winter. This way, the catkins will open and release their pollen, fertilising the female flowers that grow at the tips of the buds.

Hare

European rabbit

5

House sparrows often travel in small flocks.

6

The hare is a champion runner! Pursued, it can maintain a speed of 50 km/h for several kilometres. It lives alone, and a simple hollow in a furrow or among dead leaves suffices as a shelter. Wild rabbits on the other hand, live in colonies within underground burrows that have branched tunnels.

7

There are always flowers in every season. Even in winter, small spots of colour here and there show that some flowers can survive the cold.

Flowers of the Month

Shepherd's purse

Chickweed

Common groundsel

Stripped of their leaves, the bare trees reveal their structure, and the graceful shape of their branches.

Black poplar

White willow

Alder

Ash

Field maple

Lime

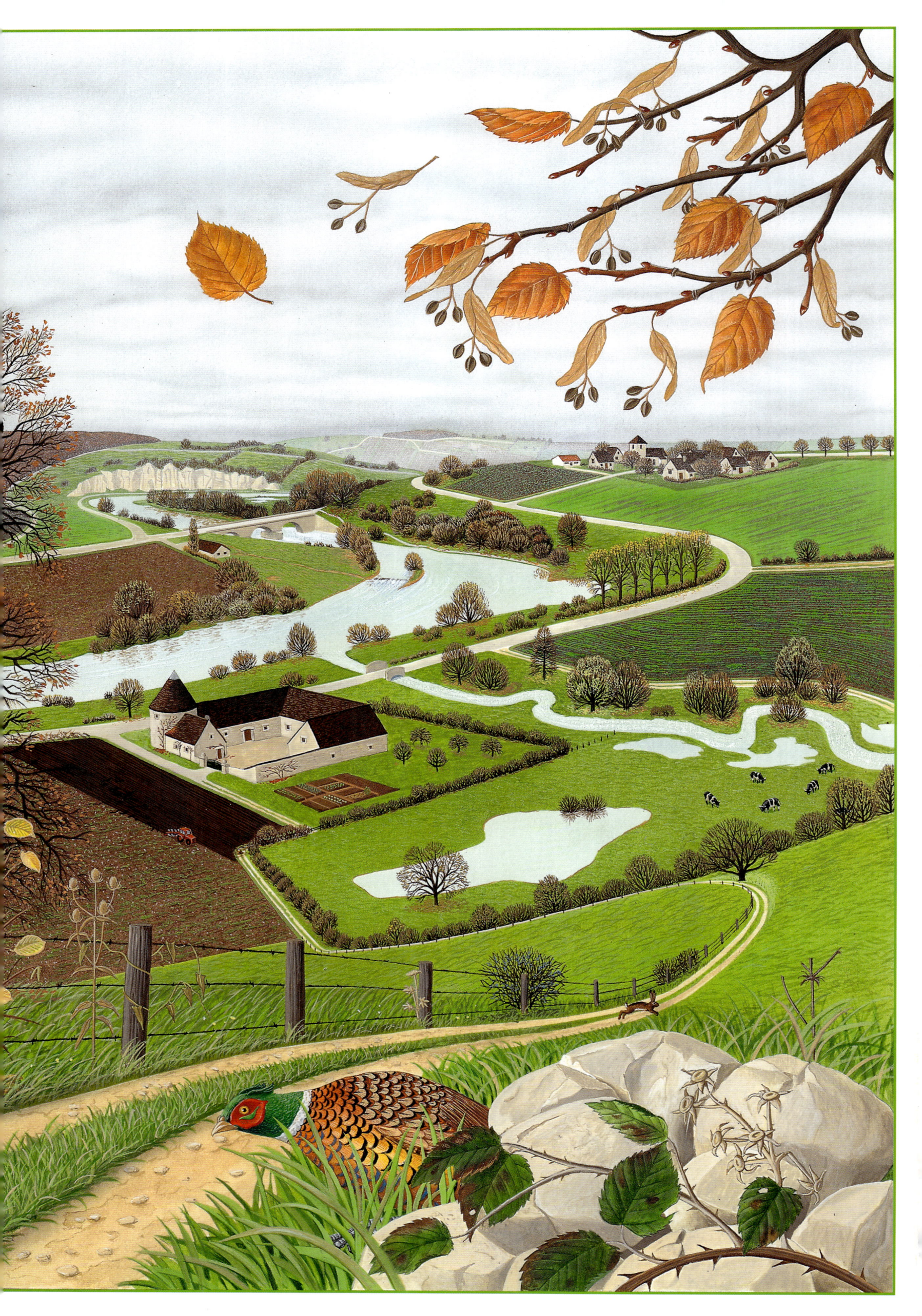

A Year in Nature: Month by Month

January 14th
3pm

February 17th
12pm

May 17th
9am

June 16th
7pm

September 14th
8am

October 17th
2pm

A Year in Nature: Month by Month

March 16th
10am

April 15th
4pm

July 14th
5pm

August 15th
8pm

November 16th
11am

December 15th
1pm

Index

K

Katydid: July
Kestrel: September
Kentucky blue grass: June

L

Ladybird: June
Lapwing: March
Lesser celandine: March
Lime tree: December
Lime tree (buds): March
Lime tree (flower): June
Lime tree (fruit): November
Lime tree (leaf): April
Little owl: August
Locust: July

M

Magpie: February
Metamorphosis: June
Mice: August
Mistle thrush: January
Mistletoe: January, December
Mole: October

O

Oriole: May
Owl: August

P

Peacock butterfly (caterpillar): June
Pansy: March
Pedunculate oak (acorn): November
Pedunculate oak (buds): March
Pedunculate oak (leaf): April
Pheasant: November
Pine marten: October
Poplar (buds): March
Poplar (leaf): April
Primula veris: March
Pussy willow: March

R

Rabbit (footprints): February
Rabelera: April
Rapeseed: April, July, December
Rat: August
Red admiral: June
Red-backed shrike: August
Red deadnettle: April
Red-legged partridge: September
Red squirrel: October
Robin: January
Rook: November
Rye: July

S

Sand lizard: July
Scabiosa: June
Seven-spot ladybird: June
Shepherd's purse: December
Skylark: June
Slow worm: July
Sloe berries: October
Small tortoiseshell butterfly: June
Snowflake: January
Soft wheat: July
Southern wartbiter: July
Spear thistle: June

Speedwell: March
Spider web: September

Starling: October
Stoat: February
Sunflower: July, September
Swallowtail butterfly: June
Swift: April

T

Tawny owl: August
Teasel: August
Thrush: January
Timothy grass: June
Two-spot ladybird: June

U

Umbellifers: July

V

Viper's bugloss: May
Violet: March
Vole: February, August

W

Walnut (buds): March
Walnut (leaf): October
Wasp: May
Weasel: February
Wheat: May, July, December
Whinchat: April
White willow: December
White willow (leaf): April
Whitethorn (*see* Hawthorne)
Wild carrot: July
Wild rose: June

Y

Yellow bunting: February